Hey Jack!

The Bumpy Ride
first published in 2013
this edition published in 2017 by
Hardie Grant Egmont
Ground Floor, Building 1, 658 Church Street
Richmond, Victoria 3121, Australia
www.hardiegrantegmont.com.au

A CiP record for this title is available from the National Library of Australia.

Text copyright © 2013 Sally Rippin
Illustration copyright © 2013 Stephanie Spartels
Logo and design copyright © 2013 Hardie Grant Egmont

Design by Stephanie Spartels

Printed in China through Asia Pacific Offset

1 3 5 4 2

The Bumpy Ride

By Sally Rippin

Illustrated by Stephanie Spartels

hardie grant EGMONT

Buzzing with excitement

Huge grin

Tingly toes

Fizzy Mood

Chapter One

This is Jack.

Today Jack is in a

fizzy mood. He is

as fizzy and whizzy

as a fire-cracker.

Jack and Billie are going horse-riding!

Jack is so excited he feels like he might **explode**.

Billie and Jack are in a holiday program. Yesterday they made pasta necklaces. Pasta necklaces aren't nearly as exciting as horse-riding.

2

Today, Billie and Jack
have dressed up like
cowboys.

It is a long drive to
the horse-riding camp.
Billie and Jack sit at
the back of the bus.
They sing a song
that they made up
with their holiday
program friends:

*'I'm riding my horse on the
range – YEE-HA!*

4

I'm rounding up all of the cows – YEE-HA!

I'm hot and I'm dusty and tired – YEE-HA!

I'm a cow...'

When they get to this bit, the boys sing 'BOY!' and the girls sing 'GIRL!' as **loudly** they can.

The holiday program leaders, Cindy and Kwan, are at the front of the bus.

'OK, kids,' Cindy says. 'Maybe you can sing something quieter now?'

Jack and Billie **giggle**.

Finally they get to the horse-riding camp. Jack and Billie get off the bus.

6

Then they all go
together to the stables.
Jack is so excited that he
runs the whole way.

A man on a big black horse **trots** over.

'Hey there!' he says.

'My name is Jim. And this is my horse, Lightning.' He swings down onto the ground.

Wow. He looks super cool! Jack thinks. *Just like a real cowboy.*

'So, who's ridden a horse before?' Jim asks.

10

Billie puts up her hand.
So do lots of other
kids. Jack begins to feel
worried. He's never
ridden a horse before.

Jim matches everyone
with a horse. Billie gets
a speckled grey horse
called Fury. It looks cool.
Billie looks very proud.

'Anybody not have a horse yet?' Jim calls out.

Jack puts up his hand.

'Not me,' he says quietly.

'I haven't ridden before.'

'That doesn't matter,

mate!' Jim says. He pats

Jack's shoulder. 'I have

just the horse for you.'

Jim takes Jack over to

the last stable.

13

Inside is a brown horse with a **fat** belly. She is munching straw.

'This is Betty,' says Jim. 'She'll be perfect for a beginner.'

Jack sighs. He was hoping for a big black horse like Lightning. Or at least a speckled grey horse like Fury.

14

Not a fat brown pony

called Betty!

Chapter Two

Jim helps everyone put
a saddle on their horse.
Jack and Jim can hardly
do Betty's saddle up
because she is so fat!

Finally they get it done.

But now Jack is feeling

very hot and **dusty**.

Next, Jim tells Jack to

lead Betty out of the

stable. Billie's horse

trots out easily. But

stubborn old Betty

won't budge!

Jack looks up at Jim.
'Can't I have a different
horse?' he whispers.

Jim chuckles. 'Betty
is a good pony, mate.
Trust me.'

No, she's not, Jack thinks. *I
got the* **worst** *pony of all!*

Jim helps Jack lead
Betty outside. Everyone
is waiting for them.
Jack sighs.

19

Jim shows them how
to get on a horse.
He puts his left foot
in the stirrup, and then
swings his right leg
over Lightning's back.

'Now you try,' says Jim.

Jack puts one foot in the
stirrup. Then he hops up
and down for a minute.

He is feeling a little

nervous.

Just as he is about to
swing his other foot over,
Betty trots forward. Jack
falls onto his bottom.
Right in the mud!

Everyone laughs. Jack
feels his cheeks get **hot**
with embarrassment.

'Not to worry!' says
Jim, helping Jack up.
'You look like a real
cowboy now. You'll
never see a clean
cowboy, that's for sure!'

'I guess,' mumbles Jack.

Finally he gets onto Betty's back.

All the horses start moving forwards. Billie's horse moves very **quickly**. It tries to get up to the front.

'Wait for me!' Jack calls.

'I can't help it!' Billie calls back. 'Sorry!'

Betty trudges along at the very back of the line. Sometimes she even stops to munch on grass.

'Oh, you are SO annoying!' Jack says. 'I wish I had Billie's horse!'

He tries to make Betty go faster, but she just goes at her own pace.

Jim takes them for a ride through the bush. They go up hills and down hills. They even **splash** through a stream!

Jack feels annoyed that he has the slowest horse, but he still has a good time.

28

Jack tries to see where Billie is, but she's too far ahead. Suddenly he hears her cry out.

Oh no, Jack thinks. *Billie's in trouble!*

Chapter Three

Betty and Jack finally
catch up to Billie. Jim is
holding Billie's horse by
the reigns. Its eyes are
white and **wild**.

31

Jack hops off Betty.

Billie has dirty tears all down her cheeks. Cindy is kneeling next to her.

When Billie sees Jack,
she bursts into tears again.

'What happened?'
Jack asks.

Kwan frowns. 'Billie's
horse isn't behaving
today. She got a
fright and tipped
poor Billie off.'

Oh, how scary! Jack

thinks. *I'm glad I wasn't*

riding her horse.

Billie shows Jack a big muddy scrape all down one arm.

'I said I would ride back with Billie to help her clean up,' Cindy says. 'But Billie is too scared to get back onto her horse.

And Jim needs to look after the group.'

'We need someone with a nice gentle horse who can go with Cindy and Billie,' explains Kwan.

Jack looks at Jim.

Jim smiles and nods.

'I'll do it!' Jack says.
'Billie can ride with me.'

'That's very kind of
you, Jack,' says Cindy.
'Are you sure your
horse won't do anything
silly?'

Jack leans over and pats
Betty's mane.

'Nah,' he says. 'Betty
wouldn't hurt a fly.
Would you, girl?'
Then he looks back at
Jim, who winks at him.

'Thanks, Jack,' says Billie. She wipes her eyes on her sleeve.

Cindy helps Billie up onto Betty's saddle behind Jack. Betty stands very still. Jack is sure she understands that she needs to be on her best behaviour.

'Good girl,' he says
quietly.

'I knew you and
Betty would make
a good team,'
Jim says, watching.
'I keep her for
special people.
And, like me, Betty
can always spot a
true cowboy when
she sees one.'

Jack grins. Even though he is hot and dusty and dirty, he has never felt so proud.

Hey Jack! The Crazy Cousins By Sally Rippin

Hey Jack! The Scary Solo By Sally Rippin

Hey Jack! The Winning Goal By Sally Rippin

Hey Jack! The Robot Blues By Sally Rippin

Hey Jack! The Worry Monsters By Sally Rippin

Hey Jack! The New Friend By Sally Rippin

Hey Jack! The Worst Sleepover By Sally Rippin

Hey Jack! The Lost Reindeer By Sally Rippin

Hey Jack! The Circus Lesson By Sally Rippin

Hey Jack! The Bumpy Ride By Sally Rippin

Hey Jack! The Top Team By Sally Rippin

Hey Jack! The Playground Problem By Sally Rippin

Hey Jack! The Best Party Ever By Sally Rippin

Hey Jack! The Big Adventure By Sally Rippin

Hey Jack! The Bravest Kid By Sally Rippin

Hey Jack! The Toy Sale By Sally Rippin

Hey Jack! The Other Teacher By Sally Rippin

Hey Jack! The Party Invite By Sally Rippin

Hey Jack! The Extra-special Group By Sally Rippin

Hey Jack! The Star of the Week By Sally Rippin